Y0-EHY-992

The Truly Remarkable Day

written by Carol Greene
art by Gordon Willman

Publishing House
St. Louis   London

Juv
G793
Tru

FOR MICHELE RAST

Concordia Publishing House, St. Louis, Missouri
Concordia Publishing House Ltd., London, E. C. 1
Copyright © 1974 Concordia Publishing House
ISBN 0-570-03424-8

MANUFACTURED IN THE UNITED STATES OF AMERICA

Once there was an olive tree and on that olive tree was an olive leaf and under that olive leaf was a small brown hump and in that small brown hump was Aggie. Aggie was a fuzzy green caterpillar. At least she was when she crawled into the hump and went to sleep. But that was a long time ago, and now it was a long time later and Aggie was finally waking up.

CONCORDIA COLLEGE LIBRARY
BRONXVILLE, N.Y. 10708

"What a lovely nap," she said as she uncurled herself up.

"Hello, world," she said as she crawled out of the hump and up onto the olive leaf to tidy her green fuzz.

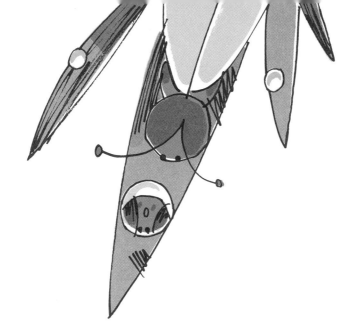

"Good grief!" she said as she looked at her reflection in a dewdrop. "Where is my beautiful green fuzz?"

It was all gone, it certainly was. There was not a speck of green fuzz on Aggie.

"What are these . . . these *dofloppers* on my back?" she asked as she looked over her shoulder.

Suddenly she remembered something from a day a long time ago before she took her nap. She had been talking to Willibald, an old worm who everyone said was very wise.

"One day, Aggie," Willibald had said on that long ago day, "you will go to sleep, and then a long time later you will wake up and be more beautiful and happy than you can imagine. "And," he had added, "you will have wings."

Aggie had laughed at Willibald. "Don't be silly!" she had said. "I am happy right now and I am beautiful too. Just look at all my lovely green fuzz! I simply couldn't be any happier or more beautiful."

Now she wondered if Willibald had been right after all.

Slowly she stretched one of those dofloppers on her back out and out till it tingled. Then the other. Then, holding tightly to the edge of the olive leaf with all of her toes, she fluttered both dofloppers together-apart one hundred times.

"They certainly feel like wings," she muttered when she had finished fluttering. "They look like wings too. They *are* wings, they most certainly are! I declare, I believe I am a butterfly. How beautiful! How happy!"

She looked around. "The whole world seems to be more beautiful and more happy today," she said. "I wonder why. I think I will try out these new wings and go see my old friends and show them my new butterfly self and ask them why today seems so special."

And as she flew Aggie sang a little song that went like this:

When I went to sleep the whole world had turned gray
And I was a fuzzy green thing.
But now here I am butterflying away.
I cannot help wanting to sing, I can't.
It's such an incredible day, it is,
A truly remarkable day, indeed,
Though why I'm not sure I can say,
Though why I'm not sure I can say.

Aggie's first stop was at a hole in the ground. "Are you home, Willibald?" she called into the hole. "It's me, Aggie."

"Hello, Aggie," said Willibald, poking his head out of the hole. "I'll join you in a minute. I'm making a scrambled egg sandwich. Would you like one?"

"Yes," said Aggie who had had no breakfast and was really very hungry.

Soon she and Willibald were munching scrambled egg sandwiches and talking about the beautiful new Aggie and the truly remarkable day.

"I knew this would happen to you, Aggie," said Willibald as he brushed the crumbs from his whiskers. "But I do not know why today is so special all over. I agree that it is quite special, but I simply do not know why. If you find out, please come back and tell me."

"All right," said Aggie. As she flew away she heard Willibald's croaky old voice start to sputter. He was singing her song, but he had put his own words to it. This is how it went:

I'm wise Willibald and I thought I could say
I'd thought every thought to be thought.
But when my old eyes see this wonderful day
I suddenly think I have not, no sir.
It's such an incredible day, by George,
A truly remarkable day, and so
I'm thinking in quite a new way,
I'm thinking in quite a new way.

Meanwhile Aggie was just flying along when she saw her cousin Martha. Martha was still a fuzzy green caterpillar and she was crawling up a fig-tree trunk.

"Hello, Martha," said Aggie. "What are you doing?"

"Hello," said Martha. "I am crawling up this fig-tree trunk to take a sunbath. Who are you?"

"I'm Aggie, of course," said Aggie. "Your cousin."

"No," said Martha. "You are not Aggie. Aggie is green and fuzzy like me. Besides, Aggie is taking a nap somewhere."

"I *am* Aggie," said Aggie. "I woke up from my nap and all my green fuzz had disappeared and I had these wings. Now I am more beautiful and happy than I ever imagined I could be. Willibald told me it would happen like this but I didn't believe him. Now I do and I suspect, Martha, that the same thing will happen to you one of these days. And speaking of days, isn't this a perfectly marvelous one? Why do you suppose it is so marvelous?"

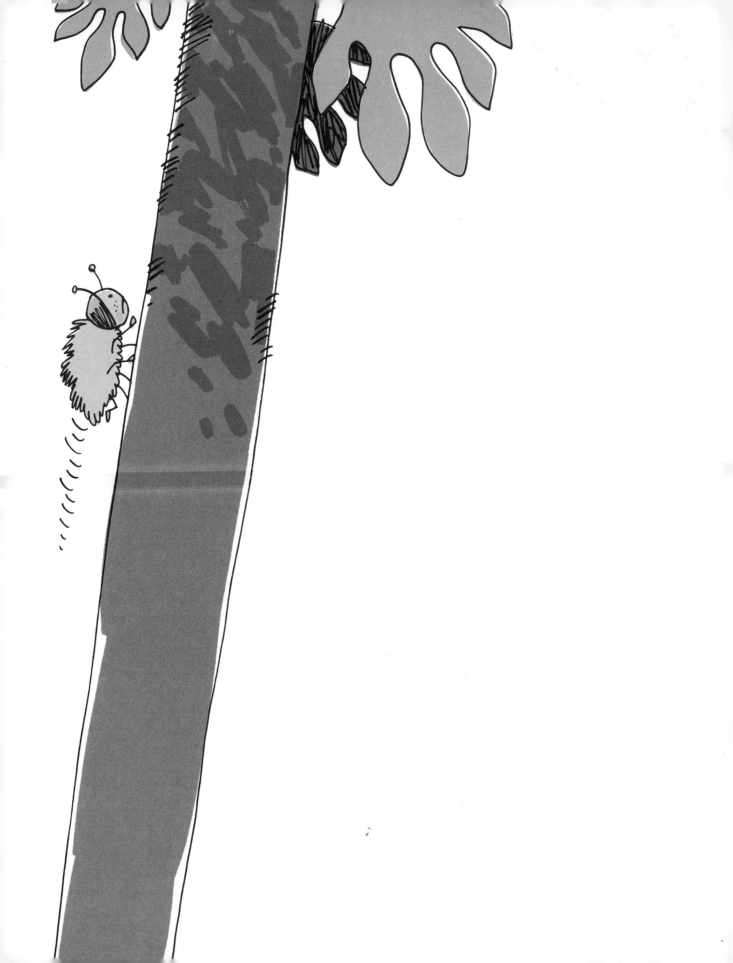

"I don't know," said Martha. "I had noticed that it is a particularly splendid day but I don't know why. And I don't believe that you are Aggie, by the way. You talk as much as Aggie but you don't look anything like her. And besides, even if you are Aggie, I don't believe the same thing could happen to me. I am as beautiful and happy as I can ever be."

"All right, don't believe me," said Aggie a little crossly. "All the same it will happen to you. You just wait."

"I'm waiting, I'm waiting," called Martha as Aggie flew away.

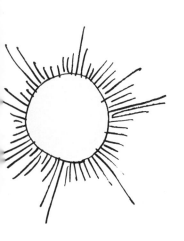

Still, a little later there came a small fuzzy voice
from the top of the fig tree. It was singing a song that
went like this:
    That may not be Aggie or maybe it may,
    But even if Aggie it was,
    In spite of how *she's* changed, I'm sure I can say
    I'll never lose all my green fuzz! And yet,
    It's such an incredible day, my, my,
    A truly remarkable day, for sure.
    I feel somewhat changed anyway,
    I feel somewhat changed anyway.

Aggie flew on and on just about everywhere to see if perhaps any of her other old friends might be there. For a while she followed a long dusty road. It was extremely dusty and made Aggie cough. So she was glad when the road bumped into a hill.

"It isn't much of a hill," thought Aggie. "All brown and empty of flowers and trees. Still, it is a hill, and at its top might be an old friend who can explain to me the truly remarkableness of this day."

So, even though it is not easy for a new butterfly to fly up a bare brown hill like that all at once, Aggie fluttered up.

When she got to the top she stopped and rested, and then she began to look around. She looked everywhere on the top of that hill, but she didn't see any of her old friends. She didn't see one living thing at all. Just some dead wooden poles nailed together and stuck into the ground.

"They are ugly, those poles are," thought Aggie. "I feel certain that they are ugly and that ugly things happen with them."

And all at once Aggie felt creepy. She didn't want to see those dead wooden poles, not ever again. So she closed her eyes and flew away.

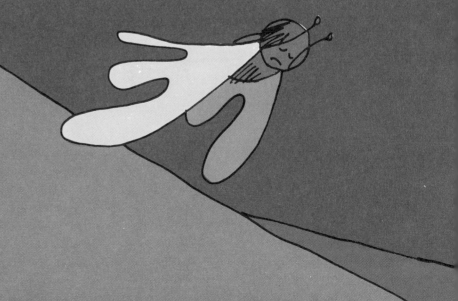

After a while she opened her eyes again, and it was a good thing she did because not two feet in front of her stood a soldier. He was clutching his head and yelling at another soldier. Aggie made a sharp left turn and floated down to a flowering bush where she could listen to them and not be seen.

"It wasn't my fault!" shouted the first soldier.

"It wasn't my fault!" shouted the second soldier.

"It wasn't my fault!" shouted the first soldier again.

"How boring!" thought Aggie. "Can't those soldiers say anything except, 'It wasn't my fault!'?"

She decided to look around. She was in a cemetery—that she could see, but it was for some reason the happiest cemetery she had ever been in. Every flower bounced and waved on its little stem. Every bird tried especially hard to sing in tune. It was, decided Aggie, a rather remarkable cemetery.

Yet none of her friends were around, and Aggie didn't think the soldiers would bother talking to a butterfly even if they had stopped arguing long enough to notice the specialness of the day. So she flew on.

And then at last she heard voices below her, young happy voices who certainly knew all about the remarkable day and were having a picnic and a very good time right in the middle of it.

"They are children," said Aggie to herself. "A boy-child and a girl-child. And although children sometimes like to catch butterflies, these two don't look like that sort of children. So I will fly very close to them and try to hear what they are saying."

Well, she did, but the problem was that the children were very excited and were talking fast, with their mouths full besides. So Aggie couldn't understand too much of what they said.

Except that the boy's grandmother had died last winter and now the boy wasn't sad about it anymore. And the girl had done a mean thing to her mother and had said she was sorry but still felt bad about it, only now she didn't anymore. And there were some other things like that.

Then the boy and girl both said together "It's truly remarkable!"

And Aggie felt a shiver run right up her back and out to the tips of her wings till they quivered and fluttered all by themselves. She understood! My yes, she understood! She certainly did! Oh, not with her brain because butterflies, even new ones, don't have very big brains. But Aggie understood with her whole self, which was for her a much better way to understand.

Oh, how she hoped she could make Willibald and Martha understand too! Even if Martha didn't believe she was herself! And as Aggie flew off, she made up some more song to try to help her old friends understand. It went like this:

When people are angry, their whole world turns gray,
And when they are sad, it turns blue.
But something has changed things and maybe I may
Begin to know what now. Do you?
This day's like a new butterfly, it is,
This truly remarkable day, indeed,
As someday the whole world will say,
As someday the whole world will say.

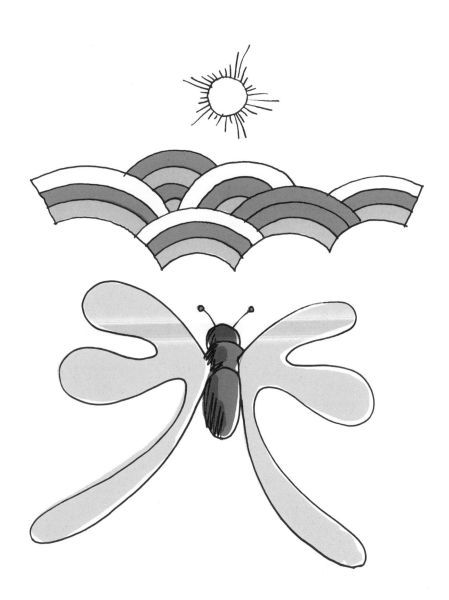

SCHEELE MEMORIAL LIBRARY

3 6655 00023558 1

G799 Tru
Greene, Carol./Truly remarkabl

JUV CPH GREENE CAROL
Greene, Carol
The Truly Remarkable Day

APR 1 8 1978   FEB 2 3 1983
JAN 3 0 1979
                APR 1 9 1983
MAR 1 3 1979
MAY 2 2 1979   NOV 7 1989
JUN 0 5 1979
SEP 2 8 1980   MAY 1 3 1994
                JUL 2 2 1994
OCT 2 1 1980
DEC 0 9 1980
OCT 0 6 1981
APR 2 0 1982
APR 2 7 1982

MAR 0 1 1983

Concordia College Library
Bronxville, NY   10708

BRODART   PRINTED IN U.S.A.